Carlos & Carmen

Over the Fence

by Kirsten McDonald
illustrated by Fátima Anaya

Calico Kid

An Imprint of Magic Wagon
abdopublishing.com

For Lisa, my writing buddy, who never tires of reading about Carlos and Carmen's latest adventures —KKM

For Bangie, my dog, who passed away early this year. Thank you for these 16 years of being by my side. —FA

abdopublishing.com

Published by Magic Wagon, a division of ABDO, PO Box 398166, Minneapolis, Minnesota 55439. Copyright © 2018 by Abdo Consulting Group, Inc. International copyrights reserved in all countries. No part of this book may be reproduced in any form without written permission from the publisher. Calico Kid™ is a trademark and logo of Magic Wagon.

Printed in the United States of America, North Mankato, Minnesota.
102017
012018

THIS BOOK CONTAINS
RECYCLED MATERIALS

Written by Kirsten McDonald
Illustrated by Fátima Anaya
Edited by Heidi M.D. Elston
Design Contributors: Christina Doffing & Candice Keimig

Publisher's Cataloging in Publication Data

Names: McDonald, Kirsten, author. | Anaya, Fátima, illustrator.
Title: Over the fence / by Kirsten McDonald; illustrated by Fátima Anaya.
Description: Minneapolis, Minnesota : Magic Wagon, 2018. | Series: Carlos & Carmen
Summary: When Carmen's wild toss sends the Hula-Hoop soaring over the fence, the twins don't know how to get it back. But then, as if by magic, their toys come sailing back over the fence. Soon after, there's a new neighbor poking her head over the Garcia's fence. Join in the fun as Carlos and Carmen meet their new neighbor.
Identifiers: LCCN 2017946753 | ISBN 9781532130342 (lib.bdg.) | ISBN 9781532130946 (ebook) | ISBN 9781532131240 (Read-to-me ebook)
Subjects: LCSH: Hispanic American families--Juvenile fiction. | Imagination in children--Juvenile fiction. | Brothers and sisters--Juvenile fiction. | Neighbors--Juvenile fiction.
Classification: DDC [E]--dc23
LC record available at https://lccn.loc.gov/2017946753

Table of Contents

Chapter 1
Hula-Hoop Fun

"¡Mira, Carmen!" shouted Carlos.
He threw his Hula-Hoop up in the air.
He put his arms over his head. The
Hula-Hoop swished down around him.

"Mi turno," said Carmen, reaching for her Hula-Hoop.

Carmen threw it into the air. She put her arms up high. "Ouch!" she said as the Hula-Hoop bounced off her hands.

"¡Otra vez!" said Carlos. "You can do it."

Carmen tried again. She threw the Hula-Hoop up. Then she watched in disbelief as the Hula-Hoop swished down around Carlos.

"Awesome!" said Carlos. "Can you do it if I'm running?"

"Yo no sé," said Carmen. "But I'm ready to try."

"¡Yo también!" said Carlos as he ran toward the back fence.

Carmen slung the Hula-Hoop toward Carlos. It soared through the air and crashed into Carlos's arms.

"Otra vez," Carlos said. "You can do it, Carmencita."

Carmen held the Hula-Hoop with both hands. She leaned back and threw the Hula-Hoop as hard as she could.

Up, up, up it went. Then it swished down around Carlos.

"Hooray!" shouted Carlos. "You did it, Carmencita."

"Double-hooray!" shouted Carmen. "Let's do it again!"

"Let's go for a triple-hooray," said Carlos. He ran toward the back fence.

Once more, Carmen threw the Hula-Hoop as hard as she could. It sailed through the air.

It sailed over the backyard grass. It sailed over her brother. It sailed over the backyard fence.

Chapter 2
Fence Trouble

"Rats!" said Carlos, peeking through a crack in the fence. "Double rats," said Carmen as she joined her brother.

Through the crack, the twins could see weedy grass. They could see the scraggly bushes around the empty house. And, they could see a lot of their things.

"I can see my Hula-Hoop," said Carmen.

"Yo también," said Carlos. "And, I can see our big, purple pelota."

"¡Mira!" said Carmen. "I even think I see our missing beanbag."

"How are we going to get our cosas back?" Carlos asked.

"Yo no sé," said Carmen.

It was a problem. A bouncy, twirly, over-the-fence problem.

"I've got an idea," said Carlos. "You can boost me over the fence."

Carmen laced her fingers together. Carlos stepped into his sister's hands. He teetered. Carmen tottered. Then they both tumbled to the grass.

"I've got an idea," said Carmen. "Let's use the deck chairs to get over the fence."

The twins ran to the deck. They each grabbed a chair and took it back to the fence.

They stood in the chairs. They stretched up high. But, they couldn't reach the top of the fence.

"Maybe there's a loose board in the fence," Carlos suggested.

Carlos and Carmen walked along the fence. Carmen pushed up high. Carlos pushed down low. They tested every board, but not one moved.

"Rats!" said Carlos.

"Double rats!" said Carmen.

"We can't get over the fence," said Carlos.

"And, we can't get through it," added Carmen.

Then Carlos looked at Carmen. Carmen looked at Carlos.

"Are you thinking what I'm thinking?" they said at the same time. And because they were twins, they were.

Chapter 3
Tunnels and Magic

Carlos and Carmen ran to the storage shed. They pushed aside their bikes and grabbed two shovels. Then they ran back to the fence.

"We'll dig a tunnel," said Carmen.

"And get back all of our cosas," finished Carlos.

The twins dug quickly. The hole got wider, and it got deeper.

The twins were so busy digging that they didn't hear the truck. They were so busy digging that they didn't hear the people.

They dug, and they dug. But soon, there were rocks and roots.

"This is going to take forever," said Carlos.

"There are too many rocks and roots," said Carmen.

The twins tossed their shovels into the hole. They slumped onto the grass.

"I don't think we'll ever get our cosas back," said Carmen.

"Yo tampoco," agreed Carlos.

"I wish we were magic," said Carmen. "We could just use our magic to get our cosas back."

Just then a beanbag sailed over the fence. It flopped down next to them.

Carlos and Carmen sat up. They stared at the beanbag in disbelief.

"What just happened?" asked Carmen.

"Tal vez, we're magic after all," said Carlos.

Chapter 4
A Pirate Welcome

Carlos scrambled over to get the beanbag. Suddenly, a purple ball soared over the fence.

"Our pelota!" shouted Carmen.

Next a Hula-Hoop twirled over the fence.

"Your Hula-Hoop!" shouted Carlos. "We must be super magic."

Carmen ran with the ball to the crack in the fence. "Carlos!" she called. "Come here. ¡Mira!"

Carlos joined Carmen, and they peeked through the crack.

28

They saw a moving truck parked in the weedy grass. They saw a gray cat under the scraggly bushes.

"I think people are moving into that empty casa," said Carmen.

"I think we have new vecinos," added Carlos.

Just then, Carlos and Carmen saw a head poking up over the fence.

"Ahoy there!" said a girl, peeking over the fence. She wore a pirate eye patch and a big grin.

"I'm Lola," said the girl. Then she pointed to the gray cat and said, "And, that's Moon."

"I'm Carmen," said Carmen.

"And, I'm Carlos," said Carlos.

"And, that's Spooky," said Carmen, pointing to their cat.

The twins looked at each other and smiled. Using their best pirate voices, they said, "Arrgh! Welcome to the neighborhood."

Spanish to English

casa – house

cosas – things

mi turno – my turn

¡Mira! – Look!

otra vez – another time

pelota – ball

tal vez – maybe

vecinos – neighbors

Yo no sé – I don't know

yo también – me too

yo tampoco – me neither